THE *DAILY BUGLE* STORIES

COLUMBIA PICTURES PRESENTS A MARVEL ENTERPRISES / LAURA ZISKIN PRODUCTION
TOBEY MAGUIRE "SPIDER-MAN" 2" KIRSTEN DUNST JAMES FRANCO ALFRED MOLINA ROSEMARY HARRIS DONNA MURPHY
MUSIC BY DANNY ELFMAN EXECUTIVE PRODUCERS STAN LEE KEVIN FEIGE EXECUTIVE PRODUCER JOSEPH M. CARACCIOLO BASED ON THE MARVEL COMIC BOOK BY STAN LEE AND STEVE DITKO
SCREEN STORY BY DAVID KOEPP AND ALFRED GOUGH & MILES MILLAR SCREENPLAY BY ALVIN SARGENT PRODUCED BY LAURA ZISKIN AVI ARAD DIRECTED BY SAM RAIMI

MARVEL   SPIDER-MAN CHARACTER ® & © 2004 MARVEL CHARACTERS, INC. ALL RIGHTS RESERVED.   sony.com/Spider-Man   COLUMBIA PICTURES

SPIDER-MAN 2

THE *DAILY BUGLE* STORIES

Adaptation by Jacob Ben Gunter
Based on the Motion Picture
Screenplay by Alvin Sargent
Screen Story by David Koepp and
Alfred Gough & Miles Millar
Based on the Marvel Comic Book
by Stan Lee and Steve Ditko

🔲 HarperFestival®
A Division of HarperCollinsPublishers

INTRODUCTION

The *Daily Bugle* is one of the biggest and best-known newspapers in all of New York City. The publisher is J. Jonah Jameson, although many of his editors simply call him "J. J." or even "J. J. J." Jameson also writes many of the editorial and opinion pieces that run in the *Daily Bugle*. He believes that he is fair-minded and truthful about everyone and everything . . . including Spider-Man. We're going to leave it to you to decide just how fair he is.

Many reporters in the *Daily Bugle* write about all kinds of things that go on in and around New York City. They report about everything from crime to the theater to science. Plus there are columns, such as "Dear Lotta" (where people who have problems can write to a woman named Lotta Nurve, who tells them what they should do to make

their lives better) and a gossip columnist whose name is Rhoda Rooter. (Rhoda goes around town, finds out what famous people are up to, and writes about it.) There's also a young man named Peter Parker who works for the *Daily Bugle* but doesn't write for it. Instead he takes pictures, and most of the pictures he takes are of Spider-Man.

(Now this part is a secret. It's going to have to stay between us. If you happen to meet J. Jonah Jameson or one of his reporters, don't tell them because that would wreck everything. See, the fact is that Peter Parker actually *is* Spider-Man. When he's taking pictures of Spider-Man, he's really taking pictures of himself and then getting Jonah Jameson to buy them. Pretty sneaky and pretty clever, right? If Jameson ever found out, he'd be furious. So nobody on the *Bugle* staff can ever find out. Don't even show them this book. You can show it to your parents and your friends, as long as they don't work for the *Daily Bugle*, either.)

In this book, we are printing a collection

of articles that are taken right out of the *Daily Bugle*. They talk about all sorts of things that were going on in New York City earlier this year, many of them having to do with Spider-Man, as well as friends of his, such as Mary Jane Watson, a girl who he's liked for a long time, and Harry Osborn, who is Peter Parker's best friend but doesn't like Spider-Man all that much. (Remember, no one knows that Spider-Man and Peter Parker are the same person.) Plus there are also stories about a man named Dr. Otto Octavius, a very intelligent scientist who works on an invention that goes very, very wrong.

Enjoy the stories and remember: Read newspapers!

WHY SPIDER-MAN IS A MENACE

Editorial by J. Jonah Jameson

(Published April 1, 2004)

For months now, this city has been held in a grip of terror, thanks to the activities of one man. No one knows his true name, or what his face looks like under his ugly mask. All we know for sure is one thing: When he shows up, trouble is never very far behind.

His name—or at least the name we call him—is Spider-Man.

There are some people in this city who are crazy enough to think he is a hero. Yes, that's right, a hero. A man who runs around in blue tights, swings from thin ropes that look like spiderwebs, and spends his days getting into fights with criminals. Criminals! Don't we have police officers in this town? Don't we have people who are paid to do this sort of thing? Where does Spider-Man get off, sticking his masked nose into police business?

And he gets in the way of fire fighters as well. Last year, a building was on fire. Brave fire fighters were risking their lives, doing what they could to help people. And what did Spider-Man do? He rushed into a burning building and "saved" children from the flames! How do we know he didn't start it? He could have, you know. Spider-Man could have started that fire right up himself, just so he could look like a hero to the citizens of New York.

If Spider-Man were really one of the good guys, why would he be hiding behind a mask? Police officers don't hide behind masks. Neither do fire fighters. Why? Because they're good. Only the bad guys wear masks so that, if and when they break the law, no one can ever find them to arrest them. Spider-Man wears a mask. So ask yourself: Does that make him the good guy or the bad guy?

The answer is obvious, isn't it?

And as long as Spider-Man runs around,

supposedly saving people and asking for nothing in return, we here at the *Daily Bugle* will be watching and telling you why everything he does is wrong.

KIDNAP ATTEMPT ON FAMOUS SCIENTIST STOPPED

Spider-Man Reported to Have Saved Scientist's Life

By Ned Leeds,
Staff Reporter

(Published April 2, 2004)

One of the strangest kidnappings in the city's history happened yesterday when a man in flying armor tried to abduct noted scientist Dr. Otto Octavius near the university campus.

Octavius had been invited to the campus by Dr. Curt Connors, a long-time professor on the university staff.

"I had asked him to come and lecture to my class about his scientific advancements," said Connors. "He's done so much to help people, and my students were very excited

about hearing him lecture."

Instead of a lecture, however, Octavius was the victim of a shocking kidnap attempt. As he walked along the street with long-time friend Connors, a man described as wearing robot-like armor and being nearly ten feet tall dropped down from overhead. According to reports, he scooped up Octavius and flew into the sky with him.

"I've never seen anything like it," said student Ariel Leela. "I thought I was watching a movie about giant robots or something!"

The man inside the armor was later identified by police as one Jack Albright, a long-time soldier of fortune who is known for his robot-making skills. Albright kidnapped Octavius for reasons that are still not entirely clear.

What is known is that the masked adventurer known as Spider-Man jumped into the middle of the kidnapping attempt. Spider-Man's purpose for being near the university is unclear.

The robot, under Albright's control, started to fly away with Octavius safely secured in a large compartment. But Spider-Man leaped aboard before it could get away.

According to witnesses, Spider-Man struggled fiercely with the robot in a fight that often seemed like he would lose.

"I have no idea how Spider-Man managed to hold onto that robot," said Connors. "His ability to stick to anything is amazing. Plus he used that fantastic webbing of his to gum up the robot's inner works."

The robot sailed wildly through the air, with Spider-Man repeatedly hitting the killer machine until he actually managed to rip through the robot's outsides and get to Albright, who was inside and operating it the entire time. In pulling Albright out of the robot, Spider-Man sent the entire machine crashing to the ground. Fortunately, Octavius was unharmed from the rough landing.

Spider-Man webbed up the angry

Albright, leaving him hanging upside down from a lamppost so that the police could capture him minutes later. Octavius was very shaken up, and decided not to lecture at Connors's class. Octavius had no comment as to why the man, Albright, had attacked him and did not make himself available to the press for comments.

Albright was taken to police headquarters and questioned. According to sources, Albright was heard to say, "Octavius has these arms he's making. . . . They can be incredible weapons. . . . I wanted his arms," before deciding to say nothing else until he spoke to his lawyer.

When asked about Albright's claims, Connors said, "I don't care what that crazy man said. If by 'arms' you mean guns, weapons, armaments, that sort of thing . . . it's impossible. I've known Otto Octavius for years. He's a scientist and not a weapons maker."

Police detective Captain Jean DeWolff, in charge of the case, put out word that she wanted to speak to Spider-Man about the attempted kidnapping, but Spider-Man has not made himself available to the police. DeWolff will continue to investigate.

THE NEW BRIGHT STAR OF OFF-BROADWAY

By Ted Rawlins, Theater Editor

(Published April 5, 2004)

The entire theater community is buzzing about a wonderful new actress currently starring in an off-Broadway revival of the Oscar Wilde classic *The Importance of Being Earnest* at the Lyric Theater in Greenwich Village.

The young lady's name is Mary Jane Watson, and amazingly, *Earnest*—in which she plays the character of Cecily Cardew—is her first major acting job since graduating high school.

"This is all too exciting for me," said the dazzling, redheaded Ms. Watson. "When I went for the audition, I was hoping that maybe I might land an understudy role. Instead I got one of the leads, and the cast

has been fantastic and very supportive."

Small wonder. Ms. Watson, with her beautiful face and sparkling blue eyes, brings a breath of fresh air to the classic play. She bounces around onstage with more enthusiasm than this critic has seen in ages, filling Wilde's words with new life. You can't take your eyes off her.

Mr. Ralph Sevush of the Dramatist's Guild, who was in the audience next to me the night I saw Ms. Watson perform, was just as enthusiastic. "I'm writing a part for her in my next play," said Mr. Sevush excitedly. "I can't wait for her to read it. I've had writer's block for six months on it, but simply watching her performance has blown it completely away. She's the greatest thing to hit off-Broadway since . . . well, ever."

Although she's very enthusiastic when talking about her acting career, Mary Jane is much quieter when it comes to her personal life. Has some lucky lad caught the fancy of this fiery-haired beauty?

"There is this one guy," she finally

admitted. "I've known him for years. Let's call him 'Mr. P.' I think he's interested in me, and I know I'm interested in him. But sometimes when he's with me, he acts like he's a million miles away. And he's so easily distracted. If there's . . . I don't know . . . a police siren, something like that, boom, the date's pretty much over. He starts getting all weird, acting like he—I know it will sound silly—like he feels he should be off helping the police. This is ridiculous. The police have their training, and if worst comes to worst, Spider-Man usually manages to pitch in and help out. Like I said, it's ridiculous, but it always seems as if he has something else to do or somewhere else to be. I'm hoping he gets over it. Heck, he hasn't even come to see me in this play."

Well, Mr. P., whoever you are, if you're reading this: Personally, I think you're crazy if you're even thinking about letting this gorgeous and charming young lady get away. Find a way to make some time for Mary Jane Watson because, I promise you,

the girl's a keeper. So go see her in *The Importance of Being Earnest*. For that matter, the rest of you go, too. And tell them Ted Rawlins sent you!

OSCORP ANNOUNCES SCIENCE DEMONSTRATION

By Ellie Mentz,

Science Reporter

(Published April 9, 2004)

Dr. Otto Octavius, noted scientist, will be making a major scientific presentation of a new invention next week, it was announced by OsCorp officials today. This presentation, according to head of special projects at OsCorp, Harry Osborn, will have many startling uses and "have a huge impact on many walks of life."

"Dr. Octavius is one of the great minds of our age," Osborn said in a press conference today, "and we here at OsCorp are thrilled to have been able to give him the money and research facilities he needed to make this fantastic breakthrough." Osborn refused, however, to give any sort of detailed description of exactly what it is that Octavius has invented. "You'll have to come and find out for yourself," he said.

Osborn did firmly deny that Octavius had created some sort of weapon, as was reported last week. "Who are you going to believe?" he asked. "Some crazy criminal in a flying armored suit, or me?"

Harry Osborn took over OsCorp last year after Norman Osborn—the corporation's founder and Harry's father—died under mysterious circumstances which Harry Osborn frequently and loudly blames on the masked adventurer Spider-Man. "I didn't come here to talk about the wall-crawler," young Osborn said, "but since you asked about it, I am still urging the police to arrest Spider-Man. I'm sure he had something to do with my father's death, and I will never stop trying to prove it."

Dr. Octavius was not available for comment about his new invention other than to say, "Prepare to be amazed. Don't say I didn't warn you, because forewarned is forearmed." After he said that, he laughed as if having made a great joke, although he did not offer to explain the joke to anyone.

SPIDER-MAN CAPTURES FLEEING ROBBERS

Helps Police in Wild Car Chase

By Ben Urich, Staff Reporter

(Published April 10, 2004)

Two men who police say held up nine restaurants in two hours—earning themselves the nickname of "The Diner Bandits"—were caught last night after a wild car chase was suddenly halted by the arrival of Spider-Man.

The men, identified as Robert Fisher, 33, of the Bronx, and Douglas Washington, 27, of Brooklyn, were spotted running out of the Malibu Coffee Shop on Twenty-third Street, waving guns and threatening pedestrians. They leaped into their convertible and sped off. Quick-thinking witnesses phoned in the

19

license plate number to the police, and the alleged thieves were soon spotted by a police car, which gave chase.

Two more police cars entered the pursuit as the convertible sped into Greenwich Village. Pedestrians scrambled to get out of the way as the fleeing suspects smashed through anything that got in their path.

At the point where it seemed that the convertible was going to elude police pursuit altogether, Spider-Man appeared out of nowhere.

"When I saw him, my pulse started racing!" said eyewitness Heidi MacDonald. "He swung down from overhead. I thought he was going to miss the car completely, but he came zipping down, straight as an arrow. The two guys in the car were shooting at him, and he dodged the bullets right in midair. I've never seen anything like it!"

According to MacDonald, Spider-Man dropped straight into the interior of the open-topped automobile. The two suspects tried to fight back, but Spider-Man was far too strong for them, slapping aside their guns as if they were toys. When they kept trying to resist, Spider-Man spun webbing out from his wrists, attaching long strands to the backs of the fleeing criminals. He then connected the web strands to a lamppost overhead, and the two criminals were yanked straight up and out of their car.

"You should have seen their faces!" said MacDonald. "Hanging from the lamppost, flapping their arms and legs around like kids making snow angels—except they sure weren't having any fun!"

Spider-Man drove off in the convertible, leaving the dangling criminals to be picked up by the police some minutes later. The car itself was recovered a half hour later, abandoned in front of the Lyric Theater.

The district attorney's office has said they plan to charge Fisher and Washington with robbery, assault, reckless endangerment, and hanging from a lamppost without a license.

Spider-Man was not able to be located by

the police for questioning in his involvement.

"Who cares about questioning him?" said bystander MacDonald. "He was there when we needed him, and he saved a lot of people!"

WALL-CRAWLING GLORY HOUND FOOLS MORE GULLIBLE CITIZENS

Editorial by J. Jonah Jameson

(Published April 10, 2004)

It seems the normally even-handed news coverage of my own *Daily Bugle* is subject to wide-eyed, foolish people thinking that Spider-Man's dangerous and criminal antics are something that should be praised and supported.

Our hard-working police officers, New York's finest, work within rules. Everything they do, every action they take, is watched by other departments that are part of the police force itself. If they so much as fire their gun, they have to fill out paperwork

23

explaining everything that led up to it and why they had no other choice. Everyone on the force knows their names and badge numbers, and they are held responsible for their actions. Plus the police have had years of training to make sure that citizens aren't put at risk when they attempt to catch criminals.

But not Spider-Man, no, no. He swings around town, masked, his identity hidden, doing what he believes is the work of the police without having to follow the rules that govern police actions. Has he had any training? Does he care about what happens to other people while he's taking the law into his own gloved hands? We don't know. No one knows. And because he hides his true name and face, no one can even ask him.

For all we know, Spider-Man is as bad as the criminals he supposedly "caught." He might have been working with them, helping them. And then, when things turned bad and the two crooks were about to be

caught by the police, Spider-Man jumped in and "caught" them himself. Why? So no one would realize that he was in league with them, to take suspicion off himself. Right now, he's probably sitting on a beach somewhere, spending the money his helpers robbed for him before he arranged for them to be arrested.

You say that I should prove that I'm right? I say . . . prove that I'm wrong!

While I'm at it, I want to respond to the following letter I recently received from a couple of our younger readers:

Dear *Daily Bugle*:

We've noticed that you used to have lots more pictures of Spider-Man. But for the past few weeks, there have hardly been any pictures at all. And the ones we have seen were really old. What's happened?

Very truly yours,

Michael and Matthew David

Funny you should ask that, boys. Spider-Man didn't mind having his picture taken back when he thought he could fool the people

of this city into thinking that he was some sort of hero. Lately, though, more and more New Yorkers are starting to realize how dangerous and sneaky Spider-Man is. From what I'm told, he doesn't like it one bit. The result? He's being uncooperative and avoiding having his picture taken.

We have one photographer in particular who's always been good at getting snapshots of Spider-Man in action. This photographer, who shall go nameless, has been trying to sell me boring pictures of dogs romping in parks and old men playing chess. Why? Because according to him, Spider-Man feels that this newspaper has "turned the whole city against him."

Well, I have two words to say about that: Boo and Hoo.

We of the *Daily Bugle* have done nothing to "turn the city against" Spider-Man. All we've done is present a viewpoint that's not confused or fooled by cheap, flashy heroics. If a magician makes the Statue of Liberty disappear, would you expect us to report,

"The Statue of Liberty has disappeared!" as if it were real news? Or would we write, "Using a spectacular trick that fooled millions of viewers, a magician performed an illusion that made it look as if the Statue of Liberty has disappeared"? I think you boys know perfectly well that we would print the second version.

So, too, am I, J. Jonah Jameson, not fooled by the tricks that Spider-Man pulls on more trusting citizens. I can see through his illusions. I know what he's really up to. And as long as I can write, I'll be here telling you the truth behind his stunts, even if it means fewer pictures of that wall-crawling menace.

HE'S ALL TANGLED UP

(Published April 13, 2004, in "Dear Lotta")

Dear Lotta:

The famous author Sir Walter Scott once wrote, "Oh, what a tangled web we weave, when first we practice to deceive!" Well, I've been deceiving someone—lying to her, keeping things from her—and now I'm pretty tangled up.

There's this girl I'm crazy about, and have been for a long time. Let's call her "Jane." We've been friends for ages, but I think she would like to be more than just friends, and I know that I would, too.

But I've got this other part of my life that takes up a lot of time. I haven't told her about it, though. I really can't. I don't think she'd understand. It's not like I'm doing anything illegal. Actually, I'm helping people. Lots of people. I'm doing it in kind of a secret

way, though, and if I tell Jane all about it, I'd probably have to stop doing it. Heck, it might even be dangerous for her if she found out.

The other night I promised I would get together with her. She was expecting me. I think she was even counting on me. And on my way to meet her, something came up that I wasn't anticipating at all. There were people in trouble, and I had to help them. And I did. But it took me way longer than I thought it would, and by the time I was done, I was too late to see Jane.

I know she's really angry at me about it. I tried calling her up to apologize and explain, but I kept getting her answering machine. My guess is that she was actually there at home the whole time and wouldn't pick up. So I kept apologizing to her answering machine, but she hasn't called me back. I don't think she's going to.

So I really don't know what to do at this point. On the one hand, I believe in this secret thing I do that helps people. I know I'm making a difference. On the other hand, there's a real danger that I might wind up losing Jane completely. It won't just be that we're not dating. It could be that we won't be friends at all. I have no idea what's important anymore.

Please tell me what you think, and sign me—

—*Tangled Web-Man*

Dear Tangled Web-Man:

I think you really do know what's important. You're simply not willing to face it.

First of all, any relationship—whether it's "just friends" or more than that—has to be an honest one. If you hold back secrets from people who are dear to you, they're going to know. They may not know exactly what it is that you're holding back, but they'll know it's something. When that happens, they'll start to get angry with you because they know you don't trust them. No one likes to be told by a friend that they can't be trusted. It makes them feel bad. Worse, it makes them feel worthless.

You're trying to help people, and that's a good thing. More of us should be out there working hard to try and help others. But while you're busy helping all these other people, you're hurting the ones who are closest to you because you're shutting them out of that part of your life.

The way I see it, Web-Man, you have three choices:

First, you can sit Jane down and tell her about this other part of your life. Somehow, I don't think you're willing to do that, though. Especially because you said that it might be "dangerous" for her. That makes it sound to me like you're wrapped up in some pretty serious things.

The second choice is that you simply drop Jane from your life completely. Decide once and for all that this thing you do, whatever it is, is more important than Jane is. If you're going to break her heart in that way, then I suggest you make it a clean break. Tell her you can't see her anymore, that you have other things going on in your life that

prevent it, and that's that. Walk away from her and keep on walking. But I don't think you want to do that, either. Why? Because if that were a possibility, then you wouldn't be writing to me asking how to fix things.

Which brings us to the third choice: You give up that part of your life that is messing up everything else.

You walk away from it. You decide that this isn't for you anymore. You say to yourself, "Jane is more important to me than anything. I'll still help people when I can, but I'm not going to ditch Jane or disappoint her anymore. She comes first." Once you've done that, you go back to Jane, tell her that she's going to be number one with you from now on, and then you stick to it.

Everyone wants to feel needed. Not only that, but every woman wants to believe that she is the most important thing in her boyfriend's or husband's life, that he can't live without her. That's how you need to make her feel, and if this secret part of your life is stopping you from doing that, then

you're going to have to decide which is more important: your secret life, or her. And no one can make that decision but you.

Best of luck, Tangled Web-Man, and tell me how it all works out for you.

—*Lotta*

DISASTER ROCKS OCTAVIUS'S SCIENCE DEMONSTRATION

"It Was Spider-Man's Fault," Says OsCorp Chief

By Ellie Mentz,
Science Reporter

(Published April 14, 2004)

A demonstration of a startling and amazing new device created by Dr. Otto Octavius ended in disaster yesterday. Dozens of watching scientists were nearly killed, and Spider-Man was said to be partly, even entirely, responsible.

Octavius was the subject of much discussion in early April when Jack Albright attempted to kidnap him. Albright claimed his reason for doing so was Octavius's work on "arms," leading to speculation that Octavius was involved in some sort of weapons design. This claim was firmly denied by Harry Osborn, head of OsCorp, the research corporation that has supported Octavius's experiments.

Yesterday the reason for the confusion was finally revealed.

The demonstration began routinely enough, at Octavius's laboratory in Flushing, Queens. Scientists were packed in and buzzing with speculation as to what Octavius had in store.

Peter Parker, a college student and part-time *Daily Bugle* photographer, spoke highly of Octavius. "Mostly I'm here to support Harry Osborn, my best friend," said Parker. "But I'm also a huge fan of Dr. Octavius and his research. I was planning to write a paper about him for my science class at the university."

Showing a flair for drama from the very beginning, Octavius came out to greet the audience after an enthusiastic introduction by Osborn, who stated, "I've known one other man in my life who I would call a true genius, and that was my late father, Norman Osborn. We can only hope that Dr. Otto Octavius will do for the people of New York everything that Norman Osborn did, and more." Octavius was accompanied by a large machine that he kept under a drape.

After a few more opening remarks, Octavius announced, "Behold . . . the future!" and yanked open the drape to reveal his invention: four long tubes, each about six feet long. They looked like vacuum hoses or, to the more imaginative, they bore a strong resemblance to tentacles made of metal. There were clawlike grips at the end of each one. They were attached to a body harness, with the four tentacles protruding from the back, and the harness was mounted upon the machine.

With complete confidence and displaying an utter lack of fear, Octavius referred to the snakelike armature as his "smart arms." In Octavius's opinion, the arms could be put to a virtually unlimited range of uses. As he strapped himself into the harness, he called out, "Imagine multitasking being taken to a new level! A lead surgeon could perform surgery completely on his own, each arm acting as if it were a member of a flesh-and-blood operating team. Or for law enforcement. No police officer would ever have to worry about being outnumbered by a street gang."

Many scientists appeared doubtful as Octavius continued, "Or if a terrorist has left a bomb and an expert has to defuse it, the expert can direct the arms as to what to do while he himself remains safe behind a bomb shield. And speaking of dangerous materials, imagine being able to handle everything from radioactive materials to deadly viruses, all without having to get your hands dirty."

As Octavius finished strapping himself into the harness, the arms suddenly came to "life." There was a collective gasp from the audience as the arms began to move around.

Then they began to pick up a series of small objects that Octavius had set up around the laboratory.

They did so with far more precision and care than anyone would have thought possible. People began to applaud and talk excitedly, becoming just as enthusiastic about the possibilities of the smart arms as Octavius himself had been.

"Didn't I say we were in the presence of a genius?" Harry Osborn stated, shaking his fists in excitement.

But then the arms began to move in different directions, and Octavius quickly lost control of them. A confused Octavius was heard to say, "It's almost as if they have their own mind as to how they want to function! But that's ridiculous! It's not as if they're alive!"

At that point, according to witnesses, Octavius lost all control over the mechanical arms. They flailed about, smashing through machinery and walls. The audience, only moments earlier a calm group of scientists,

became a frightened mob of people stamped-
ing for the exits. Octavius shouted for everyone to calm down. No one listened.

Lab assistants tried to help, but it was
impossible to approach Octavius to aid him,
as the arms were thrashing about far too
much. Anyone who got near enough would
very likely have had their heads crushed by
the out-of-control tentacles.

One witness claimed that, before he
escaped the laboratory, he heard Octavius
shouting, "Stop! Stop!" Whether he was calling to the audience or to the arms is not certain. If it was indeed the arms, his begging
made no difference. Spider-Man arrived on
the scene at that point.

Exactly how he knew there was a situation in development, or that his presence
could be at all required, is unclear.

"That's the way Spider-Man is," stated
Parker later on. "He knows where he's
needed and does what needs to be done. He's
a hero, despite what some people may
think."

One of the people who thought otherwise was Harry Osborn. "You ask me, he arranged for this to go wrong somehow," said Osborn. "He hated my father, and now he hates me. He won't be happy until OsCorp goes out of business. And all the while he tries to make himself look like one of the good guys when he's not."

According to Parker, who apparently was the only remaining spectator, Spider-Man sprinted across the room, ducking under the weaving tentacles. One of the tentacles shot straight at Spider-Man, who barely managed to duck out of its way.

The tentacle kept going and slammed into an electrical generator. This wound up sending thousands of volts of electricity through the tentacle, into the harness, and into Octavius himself. The scientist screamed as the electricity hammered through his body.

Spider-Man quickly went to the generator and ripped the power cord from the wall, disconnecting it. At that point, Octavius wavered a moment or two longer, and then collapsed to the floor. According to Parker, the oddest thing was that the tentacles were still twitching about for a few moments even after Octavius was unconscious.

An ambulance was quickly summoned, and Octavius was transported to Booth Memorial Hospital. It was there that doctors announced that the electrical shock had actually fused the harness directly to Octavius's spine. "It will be a difficult and dangerous operation," said Dr. Lance Isaacs, chief of surgery. "But we think we'll be able to separate the man from the machinery."

Harry Osborn was reportedly in seclusion, granting no further interviews beyond his initial comments at the scene of the destruction. OsCorp stock fell a staggering forty-seven points in trading. This latest fiasco might sound the death knell of the struggling company.

OSBORN HAD IT RIGHT

Spider-Man Pursues Vendetta

Editorial by J. Jonah Jameson

(Published April 14, 2004)

Harry Osborn may well wind up overseeing the collapse of the company his father started, but at least he knows his enemies when he sees them.

Let's think logically about which makes more sense. There are two possibilities:

The first is that Spider-Man "happened" to be in the area of the OsCorp laboratories at the exact moment that an unforeseen glitch in the unveiling of Dr. Octavius's new device occurred. At which point Spider-Man selflessly jumped into the middle of the disaster and managed to prevent anyone from being harmed . . . except, of course, for Octavius himself, who currently lies in a

coma at Booth Memorial Hospital.

The second is that Spider-Man has developed some sort of personal hatred for OsCorp in general and Osborn in particular. So the night before the demonstration, he snuck into the lab and sabotaged the smart arms mechanism. Then he made sure he was in the neighborhood the next day so that—when the disaster he expected occurred—he could make himself look good while at the same time bringing disaster to Octavius and ruin to OsCorp.

Which possibility makes more sense? Which holds together better?

You can believe me or not believe me. But certainly you should believe yourself, and when you look at the only two ways this entire thing could have played out . . . what does your own common sense tell you?

I call for the police of this city to issue a warrant for Spider-Man's arrest, and demand that he be brought into a court of law, unmasked, and made to answer for his many crimes. Furthermore, if Harry Osborn

ever chooses to sue Spider-Man for harassment, this newspaper and its resources will stand four-square behind him.

Only a fool doesn't know who his enemies are.

Letters to the Editor

(Published April 16, 2004)

Dear Jameson:

Only a fool doesn't know who his enemies are? How about a fool who doesn't know who his friends are?

Spider-Man is the greatest. He goes around this city saving people left and right. Is he looking for wealth and fame? No. Action is his reward. But guys like you don't get it. You have to try and find the "evil intent" behind everything he does.

You're so typical of the way lots of people think. They don't understand why someone would go risking his life for no paycheck, no nothing, but just for the sake of helping people. You figure that because you wouldn't do it, no one else would either. And if they are doing it, it must be because they've got something sinister up their sleeves.

Well, I'll tell you what, Jameson: The only thing Spider-Man has got up his sleeves is webbing. He deserves better than to have blowhards like you practicing attack journalism and writing nasty editorials. He deserves the support and thanks of a grateful citizenry.

> *Angrily yours,*
> *Flash Thompson*
> *President, Spider-Man Fan Club*

Dear Mr. Jameson:

As a New York businessman of long standing, I must congratulate you on the courage you display by calling Spider-Man what he is: a menace to decent citizens and honest businesses everywhere. I have no doubt that Spider-Man is a virtual powder keg of danger waiting to explode in all directions. From the carefully staged incidents where he appears to be a hero, to his clear belief that he is above the law, it is becoming more and more urgent that something be done about him before it's too late and he sticks his nose into places he does not belong.

> *Sincerely,*
> *Wilson Fisk*
> *Honest Businessman*

Dear Mr. Jameson:

I work on power lines for a living, and I once saw Spider-Man go swinging by while I was doing my job. He waved to me like he didn't have a care in the world. It was really obvious by the way he did so that he thought he was so much better than me. Why was he given these strange powers and some guy who really deserves them, like me, gets nothing? It doesn't seem right or fair. Man, if I had some superpowers of my own, I'd give Spider-Man the shock of his life.

> *Regards,*
> *Max Dillon*

OCTAVIUS SMASHES OUT OF HOSPITAL

Scientist Comes Out of Coma, Wreaks Havoc

By Ben Urich, Staff Reporter

(Published April 16, 2003)

An operation intended to separate Dr. Otto Octavius from the mechanical arms fused to his body came to a stunning end yesterday when Octavius came to on the operating table and smashed his way out of the room and the hospital itself.

The personnel at Booth Memorial were shocked by the incident. "He threw people around like they were rag dolls!" said the head nurse, Helen O'Shea. "I've never seen so much destruction. And we were just trying to help him!"

The operation began at 12:04 P.M. as Dr.

Lance Isaacs, chief of surgery, stood over the unconscious Octavius in an operating room, holding a saw blade. As he was about to cut into the harness that was melded to Octavius's back, the mechanical arms appeared to come to life, according to witnesses.

"One second they were hanging there, the next they all snapped up as if they knew they were in danger," said Dr. Arnold Chu, who was assisting Isaacs in the surgery. "It was like they felt threatened because they knew Dr. Isaacs was going to try and remove them."

The arms lashed out at Dr. Isaacs first, apparently seeing him as the biggest threat. They lifted him up, shook him violently, and then threw him aside. They then began to attack the other members of the surgical team. Most were knocked unconscious by sweeps of the tentacles. Dr. Chu was the only one to avoid being knocked out cold.

"I hid behind a counter and the tentacles just missed me," he said, referring to the metal arms attached to either side of Octavius.

According to Chu, once the perceived threat was gone, Octavius was wakened by the arms. He sat up and "let loose a scream so loud, my eardrums are still ringing," said Chu. "He didn't seem completely aware of what had happened or where he was. But then he started talking—his voice went low and sounded almost crazed—and then he began muttering about how Spider-Man was to blame for everything. 'Spider-Man made me look bad,' 'Spider-Man tricked me,' 'Spider-Man won't get away with this.'

"Octavius was clearly not in his right mind," said Chu.

The arms, or perhaps Octavius using the arms, smashed open a hole in the wall. He then exited through that wall and out into the streets.

Astoundingly, he was not walking. Instead the arms were actually hoisting him into the air, and he hung suspended between them. A police car arrived on the scene and attempted to stop him. But the tentacles reached over, picked it up, and flipped it over, trapping the police officers inside.

Octavius was last seen on Queens Boulevard approaching New York City. He is still at large. Police are advising that if anyone sees him they should avoid making contact at all costs and instead notify local authorities. "He is considered armed and dangerous," one police bulletin said, apparently not considering that describing him as "armed" was remotely funny.

OUT AND ABOUT

Who's Doing What, Where, and with Whom?!

By Rhoda Rooter

(Published April 17, 2004)

Gorgeous movie star Luke Charles was in town the other day, and he has an exciting new project he's bursting to talk about.

"I want to make a movie about Spider-Man!" says lucky Luke. "I've got a cast and director attached, and a terrific screenplay. And a major studio is very interested in making the film. We're all set."

Luke—who'd originally been considering bringing utterly fictional comic book heroes such as Uberman or the Sizzling Skull to the screen—naturally would play the wall-crawling wonder himself. But since no one knows who the man behind the mask is, how would that part be covered?

Luke has the answers. "Naturally we're going to take some liberties. In our film,

Spider-Man is secretly a decorated soldier and Olympic gold-medal gymnast who does all kinds of secret missions for the government. But he has a family he loves very much. And when terrorists kill his family, he uses all these weapons that make it seem as if he has the powers of a spider—suction cups on his fingertips, that kind of thing. We've hired one of the top special effects guys in the industry, Quentin Beck. He showed us all the tricks he can use to imitate Spider-Man. It is going to be so great!"

Actress Mary Jane Watson continues to be the sensation of off-Broadway as the run for *The Importance of Being Earnest* has been extended into the fall due to an explosion of ticket sales.

Yet the lovely Mary Jane's closely guarded personal life isn't fizzing the way her career is. One of M. J.'s costars in the show says that the young actress has a serious case of the blues for a young man who apparently can't be bothered to give her the time of day.

Someone get that young man a wristwatch so he can give her the time and much, much more! She's one of a kind and, young man, if you're reading this, trust me: You let her go today, and I promise you you'll be climbing the walls with disappointment tomorrow.

And that's all this go around from Rhoda!

AN OPEN LETTER TO SPIDER-MAN

From Dr. Otto Octavius

(Published April 18, 2004)

In a startling development, the Daily Bugle *has received the following letter, addressed to Spider-Man and supposedly written and sent by Dr. Otto Octavius, currently in hiding somewhere in the city. The entire letter was handwritten, and FBI experts have concluded from a detailed analysis that the letter is indeed genuine. Since the* Bugle *has no means of getting a letter directly to Spider-Man, we are publishing it here on the front page, in the hope that Spider-Man will see it.*

Spider-Man:

The usual way one starts a letter is by writing "Dear," but obviously you're not very dear to me, Spider-Man. You are, in fact, a great problem for me. You have caused me

much distress, and I'm not about to let you get away with it.

You're probably very confused by now. I know what you're thinking. "Why would Otto Octavius be upset with me? Doesn't he, like some other fools, think that I charged into his lab and saved his life?"

As if I would be foolish enough to believe that. While you're at it, why don't you try to convince me that you were one of the scientists or brilliant science students who was in the audience? This is, of course, ridiculous. That audience was filled with some of the most intelligent people in the United States. You obviously couldn't possibly be one of them, because only a madman or an idiot would run around town dressed in that awful outfit you insist on wearing.

No, no, Spider-Man. You didn't fool J. Jonah Jameson, and he has the IQ of a celery stalk compared to me, so you must realize that I wasn't taken in, either. I was confused for a while, but everything is clear now. Very clear.

You saw me as some sort of threat to you. Why, I'm not sure. Maybe because you believed I was going to be making headlines, and you wanted those headlines for yourself.

Or perhaps you were insanely jealous, because the work I do is seen as benefiting humanity, while you are seen as some sort of grandstanding freak who has only his self-interest in mind.

Whatever the reason, this much has become clear to me:

Somehow you managed to sneak into my lab before the presentation and sabotage my smart arms. That's the only way they could have malfunctioned. I am simply too great, too brilliant a scientist to have created a device that could have gone that wrong. It couldn't possibly have been me. It had to be you.

And then, when everything went wrong, you burst in like the great big hero and try to save the day. Did you intend for things to go as badly as they did? Were you planning for me to end up in the hospital, with the mechanical arms now a part of my body? Did you want me dead, is that it? Or did things simply get out of your control?

It doesn't matter. None of it matters. The only things that truly matter are the following.

First: You will not find me. But, I swear, I will find you.

Second: You ruined my dream. I will not forget that.

Third: I will find a way to rebuild. Obviously I won't be able to rebuild my laboratory in the place that it had been. The police are all over that area, and expect me to try and return there. But I will not. Instead I will obtain money, buy all-new equipment, and set up my experiments in a brand-new place.

Fourth: I will find a way to pay you back, Spider-Man—pay you back with interest.

You cannot stop me. The police cannot stop me. No one can stop me. My wondrous mechanical arms make me more than a match for anyone, including you. Especially you.

We will meet again, and we will battle. Only one of us will be left when it is over. And I can personally assure you, of the two of us . . . it won't be you. And no one, and nothing, will be safe until you are disposed of forever.

> *Yours in poisonous hatred,*
> *Dr. Otto Octavius*

The police are studying the note carefully for any clue as to Octavius's whereabouts. Octavius remains at large and is considered extremely dangerous. Spider-Man was not available for questioning.

NEW VILLAIN IN TOWN

Spider-Man Has a New, Demented Playmate

Editorial by J. Jonah Jameson

(Published April 18, 2004)

So, it's official. Dr. Otto Octavius has thrown down the glove of challenge. Does anyone have the slightest doubt that Spider-Man will snap it right up and leap into battle . . . endangering who-knows-how-many lives and guaranteeing untold property damage?

Do you notice that our city never had these high-tech or costumed maniacs running around before Spider-Man arrived? But now that he's here, they're crawling out of the woodwork . . . not unlike Spider-Man himself. First the Green Goblin, and now this, this—

What is he?

Talk to old friends of his, such as

Professor Curt Connors, and they'll all tell you Octavius is the sweetest guy in the world. They all love him. They'd lend him money. Heck, hearing the stories about him, *I'd* lend him money.

But he's not talking about money lending. He's talking about payment. And the one who is going to be doing the paying is Spider-Man.

Does that bother me? On the face of it, no. It doesn't. My sentiments regarding Spider-Man are well-known. What bothers me is the prospect that innocent men, women, and children might get in between Dr. Octavius and his prey.

Calling him "Dr. Octavius" doesn't seem right anymore. Dr. Octavius was a man of science, a researcher, a developer, and an explorer. The man who wrote the letter we printed here in the *Daily Bugle* is none of those things. He is, instead, a lunatic, driven mad by the acquisition of four additional arms . . . and, of course, by the interfering Spider-Man.

From now on, the *Daily Bugle* will be referring to the man with two arms, two legs, and four tentacles instead as. . . . Doc Ock. Doc Ock, the eight-limbed terror of New York. Let us hope that he and Spider-Man do this city a favor and get rid of each other. And let us further hope that the rest of us manage to come through it in one piece.

From the Daily Bugle *Obituaries Page*

(Published April 19, 2004)

Remembering a Loved One: Benjamin Parker died two years ago today, taken from us far too soon, through the violence of a gun, and the evil of the man who fired it. May you rest in heaven and keep watch upon us always, as we will always keep you close to our hearts. From your beloved wife, May, and your loving nephew, Peter.

DOC OCK BATTLES SPIDER-MAN

Panic Ensues at Bank as Spider-Man Disrupts Robbery Attempt

**By Ned Leeds,
Staff Reporter**

(Published April 20, 2004)

Making good on his threats to attack Spider-Man and to present a danger to anyone and everyone else in the city besides, Doc Ock— the former Dr. Otto Octavius—attacked a New York bank yesterday and attempted to rob their vault. When Spider-Man showed up and tried to stop him, a huge fight broke out that left the insides of the bank a total wreck and led to a wild battle atop the skyscrapers of Manhattan.

"It's a miracle no one was killed," said police detective Captain Jean DeWolff, in charge of the investigation. "It's clear that

Doc Ock doesn't care in the least about who gets hurt, as long as he is able to hurt Spider-Man."

The terror began at the First National Bank on Fifth Avenue when Doc Ock entered the branch at 10 A.M. He did not attract any notice at first, since he was wearing a loose trench coat over the tentacles that were hanging from either side of his body. From the moment he walked into the branch, however, the security cameras recorded the entire disaster.

With no hesitation, Doc Ock walked across the bank lobby, brushing aside customers who were in his way. As he approached the vault, which was closed, a bank guard warned him to stay back from the restricted area.

At that point, his tentacles ripped out in all directions, shredding the coat he was wearing. Realizing who he was dealing with, the guard—Carl Hogan, 47, a retired wrestler—pulled out his gun in an attempt to open fire. One of the tentacles reached

out, grabbed the gun, and crushed it as if it were made of candy. Another tentacle then grabbed Hogan by the front of the shirt, picked him up, and tossed him across the bank lobby.

This caused an immediate panic in the bank as people started to run for the exits, trampling each other to try and get out. Doc Ock paid no attention to the pandemonium he was causing. Instead his tentacles reached for the bank vault door and gripped it firmly.

"There is simply no way he could have been able to remove that door," said bank president Tom Galloway. "No way. That door is designed to be able to handle a blast from a tank at close range. When investors ask me if the vault is secure, I tell them they have my one-hundred-percent guarantee. I don't know what I'm going to tell them now."

With what appeared to be very little effort, the tentacles ripped the bank vault door completely off its hinges. Doc Ock tossed it aside, sending it toward the tellers' windows.

"I saw this huge metal door rolling toward me," said terrified teller Sandy Schechter. "I swear, I thought I was finished."

Schechter got out of the way just in time as the door crashed right through her station, completely obliterating it.

By that point, a silent alarm had been sent to the police, and sirens could be heard in the distance. If Doc Ock was at all concerned about the approaching police, however, he gave no indication of it.

Standing in the vault doorway, Doc Ock sent his tentacles reaching into the bank vault. At that moment, knockout gas was released into the vault as an automatic fail-safe in the event of robbery. But since Doc Ock was standing outside the vault, he inhaled none of the gas and the gas had no effect on his dangerous tentacles.

Within moments, the tentacles had grabbed up eight large bags of money which had recently been dropped off by the U.S. Treasury and were intended for use by the tellers. With two bags in each claw, a total haul of over a million dollars, Doc Ock turned to leave.

It was at that point that Spider-Man crashed in through the front door.

"I've never been too sure what to make of him," said Schechter. "You read all these things about him, you don't know what to think. But at that moment, I'd never been so glad to see someone in my entire life."

"When I realized we were being robbed by Doc Ock, the first thing that went through my mind was, 'I bet Spider-Man shows up,'" Galloway said. "And then, boom, he shows up. To me, it shows that maybe they're in it together. That it's all a big show on Spider-Man's part to keep people guessing."

Spider-Man did not immediately attack Doc Ock. Instead he seemed to try and reason with him.

"You don't have to do this, doctor!" said

Spider-Man. "So far, you haven't done anything that can't be fixed. Yeah, you broke out of the hospital . . . but you weren't in your right mind. If you put the money down now, admit you need help . . ."

"I already have plenty of help," Doc Ock replied. "I have an extra four helping hands, attached to four very deadly arms. Would you like to meet them?"

"I think I'd prefer keeping them at arms' length, thanks," Spider-Man told him. "Listen, doctor . . . I'm not your enemy."

"You're not?" said Doc Ock.

"No!"

"Well, that's very unfortunate," said Doc Ock, "because as it turns out . . . I'm *your* enemy."

At that point, Doc Ock began throwing the large bags of money at Spider-Man. Spider-Man leaped one direction and the other, trying to avoid them, and he almost managed it. But one of the bags hit him squarely in the chest, knocking him flat.

Before he could spring to his feet, one of

the tentacles lashed out and grabbed him by the throat. It lifted him into the air. He struggled with the tentacle, trying to break its hold on him, but didn't have any luck.

"I thought, 'That's it. He's done for,'" said Schechter.

"So I'm figuring," said Galloway, "that if the two of them are working together, then Spider-Man will get out of this. If he lived, that would prove that it's all prearranged. Like wrestling."

As he appeared to struggle against the grip of the tentacle, Spider-Man performed an unexpected maneuver. He fired a webline across the room and snagged a desk. Then he pulled it as hard as he could, and the desk skidded across the room. It crashed squarely into Doc Ock.

The desk hit Doc Ock so hard that the would-be bank robber was sent crashing through the front window of the bank and into the street.

The impact caused Doc Ock to lose his grip on Spider-Man, who dropped to the

floor, rubbing his throat. Instead of trying to run, however, he took the opportunity to charge straight at Doc Ock.

The crash through the window alone should have been enough to stun Doc Ock into unconsciousness, if not cause his body to be crushed by the impact. But eyewitnesses claimed that the tentacles managed to cushion the impact so that Doc Ock wasn't severely injured.

As it was, his sudden appearance on the sidewalk after being thrown through the window sent pedestrians running. His tentacles lashed out to slow him down, and one of them smashed a green circuit box at a traffic light, sending electricity crackling through the air.

The intersection lights instantly went out, and Doc Ock—still in motion—slammed into a cab that had halted when the light went out of commission.

Spider-Man was moving fast, leaping toward Doc Ock, perhaps hoping to take him down while he and the arms seemed dazed.

He wasn't fast enough, however, for Doc Ock saw him coming and used his tentacles to rip the doors off the taxi. He then threw the doors at Spider-Man. Spider-Man avoided one, but a moment before he leaped out of the way of the second, he seemed to realize the door was going to hit a terrified woman who seemed rooted to the spot.

"That crazy man with the arms . . . he didn't care who he hurt," said the woman, Roberta Chase. "If it weren't for Spider-Man, that door would have hit me and smeared me all over the bank wall."

Instead, Spider-Man leaped into the door's path and took the hit. The door fell one way and he flew backward into the bank.

Doc Ock then picked up several of the bags of money that had fallen, at which point two police cars, sirens screeching, pulled up to a halt. Four officers jumped out, weapons drawn. They cocked the hammers of their guns. Doc Ock reportedly stifled a yawn.

"Freeze!" shouted the nearest officer.

Obligingly, Doc Ock didn't move a muscle. His tentacles, on the other hand, stretched high above his head. They swayed back and forth slowly, and the gazes of the police officers were fixed upon them. "It was hypnotic," said one police officer, Sergeant Tom O'Reilly, who was on the scene.

Two of the tentacles began to stretch forward, and the pincers at the ends started snapping with deadly intent.

The police didn't hesitate. They started firing, not at the tentacles, but at Doc Ock himself. It didn't help. While they had been distracted by the two tentacles wavering at them, the other two had coiled around Doc Ock to create a shield of unbreakable metal. By the time the police had shaken their paralysis and begun shooting, all they were able to do was watch in frustration as their bullets bounced off the tentacle shield that had formed around Doc Ock.

The other two tentacles then reached out, grabbed one of the police cars, and tossed it on top of the other one, forcing the police to fall back.

Doc Ock then started moving along the street with amazing speed. People scattered to escape the massive arms as they hammered into the concrete with each step. One of them smashed through the top of a cab and came out the bottom, then shook the cab off.

Abruptly Doc Ock found his way blocked once more by Spider-Man, who spun a massive web directly in his path to prevent him from advancing.

"You're starting to annoy me, Doc," Spider-Man reportedly said. "This is your last chance to surrender."

"Wrong, Spider-Man," said Doc Ock. "It's yours."

One of the tentacles swiped at Spider-Man. Spider-Man leaped out of the way, and the blow pulverized the bricks where he'd been crouching a moment before. A second strike also missed Spider-Man and instead shattered a window.

"I figured it was a matter of time until Octopus nailed him," said Officer O'Reilly. "And then suddenly there was that crazy web stuff of Spider-Man's! It was the weirdest thing I've ever seen. Came right out of his arm and then it was all over Doc Ock's face!"

According to O'Reilly, Doc Ock grabbed at it, trying to pull it clear with his own hands, but was unsuccessful. Then Spider-Man yanked his webline toward him, snapping Doc Ock's face forward, and punched him in the face. He did this repeatedly. O'Reilly said, "It was like Ock's head was a rubber ball on the end of an elastic string, and Spider-Man's fist was the paddle it was bouncing off of!"

Desperately trying to regain the upper hand, Doc Ock's tentacles knocked a fire hydrant off the curbside and funneled a blast of water in Spider-Man's direction. Spider-Man was hit by the violent spray and skidded down the street before scrambling out of the way of the water blast. At that

moment, Doc Ock sent two tentacles toward him, coiling around him "like cobras, poised to strike," said O'Reilly.

Spider-Man webbed the two tentacles together, applying an even thicker coat of his webbing than he had to Doc Ock's face. Doc Ock tried to pull them apart and couldn't. So instead he used the webbed-together tentacles as a battering ram, slamming into Spider-Man and knocking him into a window.

"We were watching this crazy fight that was happening right outside our window!" said Corey Tacker, a paralegal at the law firm of Dewey, Cheatum, and Howe. "Then the next thing we know, Spider-Man comes crashing right through!"

Office workers scattered to either side as Spider-Man's body shattered the window and he landed on the floor. He clutched onto the side of a desk and tried to pull himself up.

Suddenly three tentacles smashed through the office wall. Electrical wiring and steel construction rods were ripped up

The amazing Spider-Man!

J. J. Jameson, newspaper magnate

Peter Parker tries to get Jameson to stop giving Spider-Man such bad press.

Dr. Otto Octavius unveils his revolutionary new invention.

Disaster strikes as Octavius loses control.

Mary Jane Watson, the brightest new star of off-Broadway theater.

Peter races to Mary Jane's play. Will he make it in time?

Spider-Man: friend or foe?

Doc Ock uses his tentacles to
rob the First National Bank.

Does Peter still have a chance with Mary Jane?

If only he could make her understand. . . .

Peter Parker contemplates the
tough choices in life.

Doc Ock tries to make off with the cash.

Spider-Man is back and ready to take on
Doc Ock in an epic battle!

by the tentacles as they reached about, clearly searching for Spider-Man.

A fourth tentacle came through and grabbed Tacker's ankle. "I thought I was a goner," said Tacker. But then Spider-Man snatched up one of the steel rods and jammed it through the tentacle. The pincers on the end of the arm snapped open, releasing Tacker's ankle.

The tentacle struggled to free itself. The gears inside made a series of high-pitched noises that almost sounded like screams. Green glowing liquid oozed from the puncture where the rod had gone in.

"Prepare to be disarmed, Doc," said Spider-Man.

The metal coil then went straight back through the floor, away from Spider-Man.

Spider-Man charged back out into the street, only to discover that Doc Ock had fled the scene. "He saw the police helicopters approaching," said O'Reilly, "and he got the heck out of there. Can't say I blame him. Those 'copters had enough firepower to take

down Doc Ock. Those arms of his could be made of licorice for all it would matter against the 'copper choppers,' as we like to call them."

Ultimately Doc Ock came away from the bank with no stolen money. He remains at large, as does Spider-Man. The owners of Dewey, Cheatum, and Howe are contemplating filing a lawsuit against Spider-Man for the damage he caused to the window and their offices.

WHAT DO I HAVE TO DO, DRAW A PICTURE FOR YOU?

Editorial by J. Jonah Jameson

(Published April 20, 2004)

Yesterday's disaster at the First National Bank has made it clear that Spider-Man cannot be allowed to swing free anymore.

I have been warning *Bugle* readers about this for months now, and the situation is only getting worse and worse.

A man is known by the company he keeps. In whose company is Spider-Man constantly seen? Villains. Demented madmen. Cackling enemies of decent, hard-working people everywhere.

How can it possibly be that someone such as this is allowed to roam free? How can it be that there are still those poor fools who truly believe that he's a hero?

It's becoming more and more obvious what is happening. Spider-Man is desperate to try and fool the people of this great city. So he arranges bigger, more fantastic stunts than ever before. One has to admire his fiendish cleverness. We had thought that he had done something to sabotage the demonstration that transformed Dr. Otto Octavius into Doc Ock. Now, though, it's becoming obvious that they were working together from the very beginning. Doc Ock knew that he had created an incredible weapon that could be used for crimes. Either he contacted Spider-Man or Spider-Man contacted him. They put together the fiendish plot that the people of New York are seeing played out now, in the banks, on the streets, and high above the city.

It is grand theater, dear readers. That much I'll admit. One would almost think that Doc Ock was trying to kill Spider-Man. Obviously, though, that's not the case. Why?

It's simple: Spider-Man isn't dead. The Green Goblin didn't manage to kill him, and now Doc Ock hasn't managed it. No one can possibly be that lucky. It's a game show, a stunt.

But make no mistake, it's not for laughs. There are deadly sinister motives at work. Who truly knows what their endgame is. They must have some sort of "big score" still to come, some incredible robbery in mind. It may have seemed as if Spider-Man stopped Doc Ock from robbing that bank, but don't be fooled. The money was left behind to help make Spider-Man look like the bigger hero. What's one or two million dollars when they probably have some sort of scheme that will net them ten times that?

Yes, we have trouble, my friends. Trouble right here in New York City. Trouble with a capital "T" and that rhymes with "D" and that stands for Doc Ock and his latest cohort in crime, the so-called amazing Spider-Man.

The threat is so obvious to me that I can only wonder what's wrong with you if it's not obvious to you.

MAKING THE
TOUGH CHOICE

(Published April 22, 2004, in "Dear Lotta")

Dear Lotta:

It's me again. I wrote to you a while back and signed myself "Tangled Web-Man." I had this other part of my life that was really hard, and I also had this girl I really liked and wanted to have a better relationship with, and I didn't know which way to turn or what to do.

Well, I'm not wondering anymore. You gave good advice, and I wasn't ready to listen to it. Now I am. And you wanted me to write to you to tell you how it worked out for me. That's exactly what I'm doing.

The bottom line is that this whole other part of my life that I wasn't telling "Jane" about . . . it was stupid. Crazy. Risky. Foolish. Every other bad word you can think of. It's not like people were *asking* for my help. I did it because . . . well, because I felt like I had a responsibility to do it.

But I have responsibilities to others as well. To Jane. To relatives, such as a woman I'll call "Aunt June." Aunt June has all kinds of problems of her own that she could really use me for, like moving furniture and other difficult things around the house that she can't do alone.

I was letting this one part of my life take over everything else. It wasn't fair to them. In some ways, it wasn't even fair to me.

I am tired of letting Jane down, tired of letting Aunt June down. And this other thing I was doing wasn't easy on me, either. Helping people can have its downside. Sometimes I would find myself in violent situations and get knocked around pretty good. And it was getting in the way of my schoolwork as well.

And maybe the worst of all was that the more I tried to help people, the more I seemed to get them angry. Maybe that's because I was shoving myself into places that no one was asking me to go.

So a few days ago, I looked in the mirror and said, "Enough's enough. If people don't want you to go places, then don't go there." No more doing this other job. There're plenty of other guys in the city who can help people. Police officers, fire fighters, social workers . . . people who are expected to go around helping others because it's part of their job, instead of someone like me who's seen as some sort of crazy volunteer.

I had special work clothes that I wore when I was doing this other job, but I got rid of them. I never even want to look at them again.

The minute I did that, I felt like the weight of the world had been lifted off me. The next thing I did was get in touch with Jane and tell her that things were going to be different from now on—that I was going to be there for her whenever she needed me, instead of running off at the drop of a hat; that I'd be supporting her in everything she did; and that—bottom line—I'd do whatever

it took to be the best person, the best friend, the best whatever that I could possibly be.

You should have seen the smile on her face. It practically lit up the whole room. I think I said exactly what she very much wanted to hear, but never thought she would.

If I had any doubt that this was the right thing to do, that doubt was erased when I saw her reaction.

On top of that, things are going better in school now. Because I haven't been losing so much sleep, I have a much easier time paying attention to whatever's going on in class. I'm coming up with answers when my teachers ask for them, and all of my professors are saying they see a great improvement in my work.

My life is going better than I could have possibly hoped.

Still . . . every so often, I feel this . . . I don't know . . . this pull toward picking up my old habits. Several times I've had to force myself to stay focused on my new life, instead of running around and sticking my nose yet again into things that can easily be handled by the authorities.

Then I remind myself of all the people who get so angry because I got involved in things when I shouldn't have. Plus I remember the way Jane smiled when I told her how I was changing my ways.

I still feel torn, though. But . . . I'm doing the right thing, right?

Right?

> *Sincerely,*
> *Less Tangled Web-Man*

Dear Less Tangled Web-Man:

Yes, you are absolutely doing the right thing, and don't let anyone tell you differently.

Making a big change in your life isn't easy. But there is one and only one way to handle it, and that is one day at a time. You can't be thinking, "How will I make it through the next week? The next month? The next year?" You have to focus on each day that you face when you're facing it.

That's not only the best way to do it, it's the only way to do it.

And really . . . if so many people were angry at you for trying to help them, maybe they were trying to tell you something. If they didn't want you mixing into their lives, then don't do it. No one made you the guardian angel of New York. As you said, you have family and friends who depend on you. Let them be your first priority.

Congratulations on the new direction you're taking with your life. I wish you only the best. And again . . . be sure to let me know how it all works out for you.

—*Lotta*

DOC OCK "CALLS OUT" SPIDER-MAN

Web-Slinger Proves a No-Show

By Ben Urich, Staff Reporter

(Published April 24, 2004)

Doc Ock went on a rampage of destruction yesterday in the Wall Street area. For a solid half hour, as police and SWAT teams worked to hold the villain at bay, he continued to bellow challenges to Spider-Man.

"We have unfinished business, wall-crawler!" Ock shouted as, with his powerful mechanical tentacles, he tore up the floor at the stock market. "Get out here and face me!"

Spider-Man, however, was nowhere to be seen. On previous occasions, Spider-Man has shown up at the scenes of crimes with timing that bordered on the supernatural. Not this time, however.

As Doc Ock continued to battle the SWAT teams, Spider-Man remained a no-show.

"You're a coward, Spider-Man!" Doc Ock said challengingly. "And I'm going to make sure that everyone in the city knows it!"

The SWAT teams made a valiant effort to stop Doc Ock, but ultimately were unable to do so. Although they were able to get clean shots at him, the fearsome arms always managed to come between the gunmen and their target. The tentacles brushed bullets aside and, whenever they got in range, would snag various police officers or SWAT team members and toss them around as if they were weightless.

The rampage of Doc Ock was carried on all major networks. ABC, CBS, NBC, and CNN all had reporters at the site within minutes of the start of the attack. Doc Ock, rather than harming the news crews, made a point of speaking directly into the cameras.

"You can't hide from me forever, Spider-Man!" Doc Ock snarled into a camera. "Sooner or later, I will find you! And if you wish to remain a coward in hiding, I will track you down!"

How Doc Ock would actually track down Spider-Man is unknown. He did not attempt to provide any sort of rational explanation. "I'll find a way," he simply said repeatedly.

Having completely disrupted trading on Wall Street, Doc Ock eluded capture and escaped . . . only to be spotted less than an hour later in the Times Square area. There he tossed around cars and smashed the outside of a number of theaters. He continued to shout loud challenges for Spider-Man.

Still Spider-Man refused to show up.

"What are you trying to prove, Spider-Man?" Doc Ock shouted. "We both know that you hate me—that you want to destroy me! Why are you hiding from me now? Are you that much of a coward?"

At that point, a state of emergency was declared and the National Guard was sent

in to deal with Doc Ock. Where he had simply laughed at SWAT teams before, Doc Ock had a much harder time when soldiers showed up.

As civilians were cleared out, Times Square was turned into a war zone. Heavy-duty armaments were turned loose on Doc Ock, including gas bombs, rocket launchers, and hand grenades. The fighting was fierce, but Doc Ock was finally driven away. As he fled the scene, he was heard to shout, "Sooner or later, Spider-Man! Sooner or later, you'll have to face me!"

Colonel Cary St. Lawrence of the National Guard said stiffly, "As you have seen, we had no need for some costumed adventurer to help us out. The United States armed forces are more than capable of handling any enemy . . . even one with mechanical arms."

Another officer, however, who asked not to be named, said, "I'll tell you one thing. I sure wish Spider-Man had been here. He's kind of what you would call a 'specialist.'

When certain types of enemies pop up, you want a certain type of person to come in and stop them. Spider-Man is that certain type of person."

Police are said to be searching actively for Spider-Man. "At the very least," stated police detective Captain Jean DeWolff, "we can bring him in on a consulting basis. Up until today when it took two precincts and a platoon of soldiers to stop him, Spider-Man had more experience fighting Doc Ock than anyone else had. So we figured, he's the go-to guy. But it's hard to 'go-to' somebody when they're gone."

SPIDER-MAN'S LATEST DESPERATE ATTEMPT FOR ATTENTION

Editorial by J. Jonah Jameson

(Published April 24, 2004)

It's the oldest trick in the book: Leave the audience wanting more.

Spider-Man has obviously come to realize that this newspaper and the wise citizens of New York are on to him. They've seen through his schemes, they know him for what he is.

So what does someone do in that situation?

Disappear. Vanish. Make yourself scarce. Make people think that you're needed because you're not around anymore. After

all, isn't it true that people always want what they don't have? If they don't have you, they'll want you all the more.

Give the wall-crawler credit: He knows his suckers.

"Spider-Man, save us!" I'm sure many of you are crying out. Having fallen into his web of deceit and lies, you believe that only a masked outlaw in blue and red can save decent citizens from the maniacal attacks of Doc Ock.

Well, let's look at the facts, shall we?

Spider-Man, for whatever reason, didn't show up to oppose Doc Ock. Maybe, as I strongly suspect, he's working with the tentacled terror and was staying out of his cohort's way. And then there are those of you who think that they're not working together—that Spider-Man is truly on the side of the angels. In that case, obviously his courage must have taken flight, because he was too afraid to come face-to-face with what is clearly a stronger opponent than he's used to. Either way, it doesn't exactly reflect well on him.

Consider, though, what jumped into place to replace him. Police. Talented members of the Special Weapons and Tactics (SWAT) team. And our brave U.S. military. All doing the things they're supposed to do, and all proving that you don't need a fancy costume or superpowers to get the job done. All you need is guts, which our police officers and military have tons of . . . and Spider-Man has none. Even when he's supposedly fighting to protect people, still he hides behind that mask.

Doc Ock is insane, but even a stopped clock is right twice a day. Spider-Man was a coward from the very beginning. It took a demented criminal to make that obvious to everybody.

BREAK-IN AT SHOREHAM NUCLEAR POWER PLANT

By Fred Foswell,

Staff Reporter

(Published April 26, 2004)

Government authorities reported a break-in at Shoreham Nuclear Power Plant. The security system was disabled so there is no visual record of who committed the crime.

Several small vials filled with various nuclear materials were stolen from a secure area. "No human being could have gone in there to get them. The radiation levels were too high," said Shoreham manager I. M. Glowing. "The only way someone could have done it is if he had long, powerful arms capable of ripping the secure doors right off the hinges and then

entering the rooms and putting the radioactive materials into protective boxes."

Police reported no suspects.

DOC OCK THREATENS OSBORN

OsCorp Head Questioned by Police in Connection with Late-Night Meeting

By Ben Urich,
Staff Reporter

(Published April 27, 2004)

Doc Ock broke into the apartment of OsCorp top executive Harry Osborn and tried to extort money from him, according to police who have been questioning Osborn after the unexpected meeting.

Police were alerted by long-time Osborn employee Edmund Bernard, Osborn's butler and house manager. As he was leaving for the night, Bernard spotted the invading Doc Ock as the villain approached the Central Park townhouse where Osborn lives.

"He was impossible to miss," said Bernard. "The ground shook under him every time one of those huge metal tentacles of his jammed into the concrete. It felt as if a Tyrannosaurus rex was approaching."

Doc Ock propelled himself upward and entered the townhouse through Osborn's balcony. The exact nature of his subsequent discussion with Osborn is what police are currently investigating.

Sources inside the police department claim that Doc Ock was attempting to get money from Osborn. "He has some sort of research he's trying to finish," said one source who did not wish to give his name. "Some sort of huge project or invention or something. He needs money to do it, and felt that Harry Osborn was the guy to go to for it."

Osborn and Ock have a connection to each other, ever since Osborn funded the creation of the "smart arms" that the former Dr. Otto Octavius went on to use in his criminal career as Doc Ock. Supposedly Ock

felt that Osborn still owed him some sort of debt, and that a large sum of money was the only way to even that debt.

Some within the police force conjectured that Osborn was somehow working together with Ock, since their mutual hatred for Spider-Man is well-known. It was a speculation heatedly denied by Osborn.

"I'm the victim here!" Osborn told police. "I was minding my own business at home when this homicidal maniac with metal arms suddenly comes into my apartment, right through my balcony. He threatened me! He demanded money! He said he would kill me if I didn't come up with huge amounts of cash to pay him off. It wasn't as if I had a ton of money lying around the house. Although if I had, I swear I would have given it to him. I was that terrified of him."

The question police were left with, then, was exactly why Osborn was still alive after Doc Ock departed. The speculation was that, if Osborn failed to come up with money or strike some sort of deal with Doc Ock, then the tentacled menace would have killed Osborn out of anger or spite.

"You ask me," said one source, "Osborn cut some sort of deal with him. I think what happened is this: Doc Ock threatened him. Osborn offered to pay him off if he would do something for Osborn. And whatever Osborn wanted him to do, it must have been something that Doc Ock was more than happy to do, because a guy like him isn't going to be Harry Osborn's errand boy. My guess is, Osborn asked him to make sure something bad happened to Spider-Man. Maybe even to kill him."

"That's ridiculous!" Osborn replied when told of police suspicions as to what had happened. However, even as Osborn protested, he stammered and looked nervous, indicating to this reporter that he knew things he wasn't saying. "I mean . . . I'm a law-abiding citizen. Telling one person to go out and kill another person . . . that . . . that would be against the law. And

let's say, just for laughs, that I did tell Doc Ock that I'd pay him if he killed Spider-Man. Which I didn't! But let's say I did. The thing is, Spider-Man's disappeared. So when I told Doc Ock . . . I mean, *if* I had told that to Doc Ock, I would have done so knowing that Spider-Man was going to be perfectly safe in any event."

If Doc Ock were to try and find Spider-Man, police are still trying to determine how he would go about doing so, especially considering police have been unable to find any trace of the wall-crawler since his disappearance of several days ago.

"My guess," said an unnamed police source, "is that Osborn would have suggested that Doc Ock go after someone who has some sort of connection to Spider-Man."

Osborn once again raised objections to the notion. "Oh, come on!" said Osborn. "Why would I suggest that Doc Ock go after one of my best friends? I'd never want to put one of my best pals in harm's way. What kind of friend would I be if . . . ?"

At that point, Osborn was reminded that no one had mentioned him suggesting that Doc Ock go after a personal friend of Osborn's. "Well, somebody must have mentioned it!" said Osborn, his face flushing red. When he was assured no one had, he replied, "Well, somebody was probably about to!" All of this indicated that the strain of his failing company and now this latest threat has weighed heavily on Osborn; he seems near to his breaking point.

Police are currently searching out various friends and acquaintances of Harry Osborn's. This includes people such as his former girlfriend, off-Broadway star Mary Jane Watson.

"I've known Harry for years, and he would never deliberately put one of his friends in danger," said Mary Jane Watson firmly. When questioned about Osborn's feelings on Spider-Man, however, Watson hesitated, and then said, "Truthfully . . . I don't think there are any lengths Harry wouldn't go to if it meant getting rid of

Spider-Man once and for all. I've spoken to him about this . . . this obsession of his. He can't drop his hatred of Spider-Man. If you came to me tomorrow and told me you had definite proof that Harry put some sort of price on Spider-Man's head, it wouldn't surprise me in the least. Then again, it's not as if Spider-Man is a friend of his. So that's something, I guess."

Continued efforts by the police to locate Spider-Man have proven fruitless.

Letters to the Editor

(Published April 29, 2004)

Yo, Jameson:

I hope you're happy, you Brillo-headed dope. If Spider-Man is gone, it's because he's sick of two-bit ingrates like you coming down on him 24/7. Spider-Man was the best thing that ever happened to this city, and you've got a head full of cheddar cheese if you think any different.

Man, I hope stuff happens to you that makes you regret all the stuff you said. I hope you get attacked by Doc Ock. Or maybe a guy in a giant scorpion suit. Or a robot. Or maybe your son will turn into a werewolf. Yeah, how'd you like that to happen, huh?

Creep.

Yours in contempt,
Flash Thompson
President, Spider-Man Fan Club

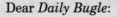

Dear *Daily Bugle*:

I run a fruit and vegetable stand not too far from the university. I opened it a year ago and in the first six months I was robbed six times. Six times. By the same people. They wore masks, but I knew it was them. And every time I was robbed, the police would come, fill out some forms, shake their heads, and talk about how sad it was. And they suggested that maybe I should move my stand to another neighborhood.

I know the police are overworked. I know there are not nearly enough of them to be everywhere they're needed. I know their job is tough. But imagine how I felt with them telling me that I should get out because it's too tough to catch the criminals.

And then, one day, the two masked men came again, and they were ready to rob me. And suddenly one of them pointed upward and yelled, and then just like that, swish, they were gone. Spider-Man had come swinging down from overhead, and he grabbed

them and webbed them up to the top of a lamppost. They hung there like big lumps of coal in Christmas stockings, nicely wrapped presents for the police.

And before he went, I heard him say to these guys, "Whenever you guys are done with your jail time, I don't care. You stay away from this stand. This whole neighborhood. In fact, if you're smart, you stay out of my city." And those guys, they were saying, "Yes, Spider-Man! Don't hurt us, Spider-Man!"

It was the first time I actually felt safe.

Those men, I kept track. They got a plea bargain, and they were only in jail for three months. Which means they have been out for three months, but they still never come around here. Why? Fear of Spider-Man.

Then you, with all your editorials, got people all worked up. And now Spider-Man is gone, and we're on our own. Yeah, he wears a mask, like the bad guys. You know what? Police carry guns, like the bad

guys. Nobody thinks police shouldn't have guns. They have it for protection. Maybe Spider-Man has a mask for his own protection. Maybe he wants to protect loved ones. Maybe he worries that if everybody knows who he is, they'll all keep coming to him and asking him for his help, so much that he'll never have any life of his own. Maybe he has pimples and is embarrassed about it.

Who knows? Who cares? All I know is, I'm worried the bad guys will come back with Spider-Man not here, and I think he's not here because of you.

So thanks a lot and I'm going to cancel my subscription.

Angrily yours,
Irving Forbush

Dear Mr. Jameson:

I have been a subscriber to the *Daily Bugle* for many years now. I've been reading it regularly since I was a little girl, and I can assure you that was quite a long time ago.

Over the years, I've watched certain editorial opinions at the newspaper change.
Recently, I've seen many editorials by you
that are viciously slanted. You obviously have
some sort of axe to grind—particularly when
it comes to Spider-Man. I can't begin to know
why you have such hatred for him. Part of me
thinks that your overriding impulse is envy.
You're jealous of him because he does things
you couldn't possibly do, with powers that
are unique while you . . . well, you don't have
either of those things going for you. So all
you can do is pick at him and pick at him, trying to bring him down to your level since you
cannot possibly rise up to his.

Now Spider-Man has disappeared. The
people of New York who used to look up and
see him flying past on his webs now look to
the skies and see nothing. And the skies seem
the emptier for it.

I read all this talk of whether Spider-Man
is a coward, and whether he's a criminal. No
one seems to be able to understand why
Spider-Man might have vanished from the

public eye. Frankly, I'm surprised. I would have thought it was obvious.

This city is filled with ingrates.

While Spider-Man was risking his life time and again, people like you, and those foolish enough to agree with you, tried to come up with all the worst reasons why he was doing what he was doing. You called him a criminal. You called him a liar. You called him dishonest. You called him someone putting forward a fraud on the people of this great city.

What you never called him was "friend." The simple truth is that Spider-Man is the best friend this city ever had.

I happen to have a couple of friends who work at the bank branch where Spider-Man fought Doc Ock. You can talk about "wrestling" and "staging fights" all you want. But these young women swore to me that, if Spider-Man had not shown up when he did and fought Doc Ock, they would very likely be dead by now. So right there, Spider-Man made sure that my two friends would be

alive to share pleasant afternoon tea with me in the future.

Then there's another young woman of my acquaintance: Mary Jane Watson, whose name has been brought up in these pages several times in recent editions. Last year, Mary Jane was kidnapped by that horrible Green Goblin. He dangled her over the river and threatened to let her fall to her death. In fact, he wound up letting go of her so that she might have done just that. So why is Mary Jane alive, well, and thrilling critics and audiences with her performance onstage?

Spider-Man. Spider-Man saved her. And he asked for nothing in return.

But even though he has asked for nothing, there's something we very well could have given him. We could have given him our thanks and our appreciation. Clearly you're never going to do that. So I will do it for you.

Thank you, Spider-Man.

Thank you for your bravery.

Thank you for the sacrifices you have made.

Thank you for the people that you've rescued.

Thank you for all the times that you've risked your own life on our behalf.

Thank you for using these strange powers of yours to help others.

Thank you for being there with no thought of recognition or reward.

I have a nephew. He's not at all like you. He's very shy, very quiet. I worry about whether he's dressed warmly in winter or wearing his galoshes in the rain. I love him very dearly. Yet for all that, in some ways, I wish he were a bit like you. I wish he took his nose out of his books every so often and saw a world that needed the help of anyone who was willing to help it.

Thank you for all you've done for us, Spider-Man. If you choose to do nothing more, then know that I and many others appreciated you, and never took the time to tell you. For that I'm very sorry. If you choose

to come back and start helping the people of
New York again . . . then heaven bless you, as
will I.

>*Very truly yours,*
>*May Parker*
>*Forest Hills, Queens*

AN OPEN LETTER TO DOC OCK

From Your Friendly Neighborhood Spider-Man

(Published April 30, 2004)
The following letter was found in the office of Bugle *publisher J. Jonah Jameson. We have reason to believe that it is genuinely from Spider-Man . . . the main reason being that, as Mr. Jameson sat down to read it, he discovered a large amount of what is unquestionably Spider-Man's webbing had been left behind in his chair. The result was that Mr. Jameson was stuck to his chair for an hour. Mr. Jameson wishes to make clear that this stunt has only convinced him all the more that Spider-Man is a menace, and this letter is being run only because we think it newsworthy rather than as any endorsement of Spider-Man's activities.*

Okay, Doc. You asked for it.

You've been going all over town, stirring up trouble. Threatening our fine police officers, smacking around the United States military. I'm sure you think that you've got everything under control. That you've got the whole world in your . . . well, in your tentacles.

You're about to find out how wrong you were.

Why was I not around to stop you before? Doc, I'd love to tell you what the problem was. I'd love to tell you about my poor, sick old mom. Or that my nine kids had the sniffles and, since their mother was working, I had to take care of the brood and play Mr. Spider-Mom. Or that my boss, Mr. Dithers, told me that if I didn't stay late making sure that the Finster contract went out on time, it would be my masked neck on the chopping block. Or maybe I was so upset over you calling me a coward that I crawled into a little ball here in the Spider-Man Cave and sobbed myself to sleep while clutching my Elmo doll.

But it wasn't any of those things,

Doc. Would you like to know what it was? I'll tell you: It was none of your business, is what it was. None of your beeswax. Not your affair. You don't have to know.

Here's what you do have to know.

I'm back.

I'm back, and I'm not going to sit around and let you smack my city or my people around anymore.

You threatened Harry Osborn. And then you went and threatened Harry's friend, Peter Parker . . . a guy who happens to be very close to me.

He was riding along on his motor scooter, just thinking about his life, and suddenly you came down from overhead and grabbed him. You shook him and tried to scare him. You brought him up real close to your face so you could snarl in his, and he could smell your very unfortunate breath, and you told him to find me. You told him that if I didn't meet you in a particular place at a particular time, then you would hunt Peter down and kill him.

He never did anything to you, Doc. Not a darned thing. Yet you were ready to kill him.

Well, guess what, Doc? Your timing couldn't have been better, because I was ready to come back, rested and all set to play. That's exactly what I'm going to do. Believe me, Doc, when I tell you that if you threaten Peter Parker, you threaten me. And I don't take kindly to threats.

So you better believe that I'm going to meet you at the time and place that you challenged me to meet you. And I'm coming in ready to show you that there's not enough room in the city for the both of us. Which means I'm going to be giving you your eviction notice.

And to all the people who wrote in support of me, and told stories about how much I meant to them . . . to Mr. Forbush, who need not worry about the safety of his fruit and vegetable stand . . . and Flash Thompson, uh, okay, Flash—your heart's in the right place, but next time, don't try to help me . . . and especially to Ms. May

Parker in Forest Hills . . .

It was appreciated. More than I think you'll ever know.

Doc, look out. Here comes Spider-Man.

DOC OCK MENACE ENDED!

Doc Ock Believed Killed in Pier Explosion

—

Police Investigating Spider-Man Connection

By Ned Leeds,
Staff Reporter

(Published May 1, 2004)

A huge explosion rocked the area of Pier 56 late last night, and police believe that it could very well have signaled the end of the menace of Doc Ock.

There were no reliable witnesses to the explosion that shattered windows for miles and caused a blackout that knocked out power throughout the entire downtown area. There were other, even more bizarre occurrences in the minutes leading up to the

explosion. There was some sort of magnetic burst so powerful that it wiped clean the hard drives of any computer within a two-mile radius, and some people who live close to Pier 56 even claimed that the walls of their apartments were bending as if being sucked into some sort of giant vacuum.

Police tend to dismiss those last accounts as being "tall tales" told by panicked residents. Scientists investigating the mishap tell a different story, however.

"As insane as it may sound," said university professor Dr. Curt Connors, "it almost seems as if something similar to a very small sun was being cooked up at the pier. That would have all the results that people are talking about. It would give off such a huge burst of magnetism that it would wipe out computer hard drives. Plus the gravity of such a thing would be capable of pulling anything nearby right into it. For that matter, if it began to grow, why . . . it could have pulled the entire planet in."

When asked if a device able to make a

small sun actually existed, Connors said it did not. "But if anyone was capable of creating something like that, it would certainly have been Otto Octavius."

Dr. Otto Octavius is the true name of the man newspapers and police have come to refer to as "Doc Ock." When informed of Connors's theories, police were very skeptical. "I've seen a lot of things in my time on the force," said police detective Captain Jean DeWolff. "A lot of strange things. But I can tell you with absolute assurance that I've never seen some sort of crazy machine that creates suns. I have, however, seen incredibly big bombs. A nuclear bomb would generate the exact kind of pulse that would knock out computers. Fortunately, we know this wasn't a nuclear bomb because . . . well, obviously it wasn't since the city is still here instead of a giant crater. What it was, though, I really don't know."

Police have, however, questioned a number of people in connection with the recent activities of Doc Ock, as well as anyone who is a friend of, or has any connection with, OsCorp special projects head Harry Osborn. "Through a good deal of old-fashioned detective work," said DeWolff, "we believe we have a theory of exactly what happened."

According to police, the following events led up to the explosive confrontation between Spider-Man and Doc Ock:

Doc Ock went to Osborn and demanded money in order to complete some sort of dangerous invention . . . presumably the bomb that went off on the pier.

Osborn refused to pay him, but, terrified that Doc Ock would hurt him, suggested a deal: If Doc Ock would kill Spider-Man, Osborn would give him the money he requested. Police believe that Osborn never thought that Ock would actually be able to find Spider-Man, or else that Spider-Man would instead be able to defeat Doc Ock.

Doc Ock, either on his own or prompted by Harry Osborn, went after a friend or friends of Spider-Man's and threatened them, telling them that if Spider-Man refused to meet Doc Ock at Pier 56, Doc Ock would come after the friends and injure or kill them.

The threats made their way to Spider-Man, who, for whatever reason, had been leaving Doc Ock to spread his reign of terror upon the city.

According to DeWolff, from there on the police description of the events becomes murky. "If only we had some reliable witnesses to tell us everything that happened," said DeWolff. "We've managed to piece together some things thanks to what we were told by a couple of bums who were sleeping in the area and woke up when things started going bad. But they'd had so much to drink, it's hard to know how much of what they said is true and how much isn't."

Not much is left of the warehouse on Pier 56 in which Doc Ock had apparently been hiding out. Police teams have gone over every square inch of Pier 56, however, and this is what they think happened in the

final battle between Spider-Man and Doc Ock.

Spider-Man approached Pier 56, swinging on his webline, being very careful so that he didn't attract the attention of Doc Ock. He landed on the north wall of the building and peered in through a loose board. There he saw Doc Ock, cackling wildly, working on some sort of huge bomb. Presumably Doc Ock was so far gone that he had decided the best way to handle things was to blow New York City off the face of the Earth. After all, he hated Spider-Man more than anything. And Spider-Man lived in New York City. So if the city went, then Spider-Man would definitely go with it.

Upon seeing exactly what Doc Ock was up to, Spider-Man decided to try the element of surprise. Firing a webline, he snagged it on the ceiling and swung down toward Doc Ock with the intent of knocking him right out. If he took down Ock quickly, he could devote his time to figuring out how to deactivate the huge bomb on the pier.

Doc Ock, however, was not taken by surprise. Or perhaps he was, but his tentacles most certainly were not.

As Spider-Man drew near, the tentacles lunged out at him. Spider-Man barely managed to get out of the way as they grabbed up huge empty crates and started throwing them at Spider-Man.

Spider-Man dodged to the left and the right, trying to get close to Doc Ock, but the arms were keeping him at a distance. By that point, of course, the full attention of Doc Ock was on him.

According to the admittedly unreliable descriptions given by the drunk eyewitnesses, Spider-Man called out, "It's over, Doc! Time to give up whatever crazy scheme you're working on!"

"You're the crazy one, Spider-Man," said Doc Ock, "if you think I have the slightest interest in anything you have to say!"

"What do you think you're going to accomplish by this?" Spider-Man asked.

"I will have shown the people of New York that they were fools to treat me the way they have!" Doc Ock told him. "They think I'm insane! Twisted! Sick! They laugh at me! But no one will be laughing at me after this. You aren't laughing at me!"

"Sure I am," Spider-Man said. "Jonah Jameson is always wondering why I'm wearing a mask. That's why. So the bad guys won't be able to tell when I'm laughing at them. I wouldn't want to hurt their feelings, after all."

"How dare you!" Doc Ock shouted, and his metal tentacles lashed out at Spider-Man.

As all four tentacles came after him at one time, Spider-Man moved with such incredible speed that the tentacles began to get tangled up in each other. Within moments Spider-Man had all four tentacles wrapped around each other in one huge knot. He then sprayed his webbing onto the knot of arms in hope of keeping them all in one place.

A daring plan, but one that didn't actually

work. The four arms pulled in four different directions and managed to tear the webbing apart.

As the fight continued, the device that Doc Ock had built began to get louder and louder. "Shut this thing down now, Doc!" Spider-Man shouted at him, trying to make himself heard over it. "Before it's too late!"

"It's already too late!" Doc Ock said. "Too late for the city, and too late for you!"

The tentacles of Doc Ock speared upward toward the ceiling and ripped what police believe to have been several tons worth of machine parts and debris down upon Spider-Man. There was too much for him to dodge, and within moments Spider-Man was buried beneath it.

"There!" Doc Ock reportedly said. "That takes care of that!"

The noise from the machine grew even louder, and it was at that point that buildings all around the immediate area began to shake violently from the vibrations of the device.

But as Doc Ock prepared to set off his

deadly machine, Spider-Man apparently struggled beneath what Doc Ock had brought down upon him. The pile of debris on top of Spider-Man began to shift. Minutes later, Spider-Man stood, shoving aside all the garbage that had landed on top of himself. His costume was torn from all the things that had fallen on him. He didn't appear to care.

"This has to stop!" Spider-Man reportedly shouted, "and you're the one who's going to have to do it!"

Opinions vary widely on what happened next. The most likely scenario, according to police, is the following:

Spider-Man leaped from one place to the next to the next, staying one step ahead of the fierce tentacles of Doc Ock. He would land on a particular place on the floor near the machine and wait for one of the tentacles to smash down at him. It was a pinpoint, hair-raising tactic to take.

The moment that one of the tentacles would come at him, he would jump out of the way. The tentacle would barely miss him and smash into the floor. It would then tear out huge chunks of the floor to free itself. Meanwhile Spider-Man would be crouching a few feet away, and another tentacle would lash out at him.

Again he would dodge it, and again the tentacle ripped at the floor in missing him. Another hole was created, and another, and still another. Suddenly, there was a horrendous creaking, and Doc Ock came to the terrified realization that he'd been tricked by Spider-Man. He had torn up so much of the flooring under his explosive machine that there was no longer enough of the pier left to support it.

The huge machine began to teeter, the remaining flooring bending and splintering under it. Doc Ock grabbed at the machine with his tentacles, trying to support it and prevent it from sliding into the Hudson River. Unfortunately, as strong as Doc Ock's tentacles might have been, they weren't going to do him any good if he

himself wasn't standing on anything solid.

In attempting to stop the machine from crashing through the pier, all Doc Ock managed to do was support too much weight. As a result, not only did the machine collapse through the pier . . . but so did its creator. According to police, Doc Ock held on to his destructive machine for all he was worth. It did him no good. Within seconds, both Doc Ock and his machine went under. Spider-Man could do nothing but stand there helplessly and watch as the two of them vanished beneath the waters of the Hudson.

The unreliable witnesses who were there presented a very different story to this reporter, one that the police have labeled as "very unlikely."

According to the unreliable witnesses, Spider-Man somehow managed to talk sense into Doc Ock and made him realize that his plan to use his machine against the city— whatever that machine might have been designed to do—was wrong. Becoming the law-abiding citizen he used to be, Doc Ock

regained his sanity and tried to shut the machine down himself. When he was unable to do so, he shoved Spider-Man to one side and sent the machine into the river himself. In doing so, he was pulled down with it, and Spider-Man was unable to save him.

"It's a very imaginative version of the events," DeWolff said. "But the men who claim to have seen that happen both drink heavily and can barely remember their own names, much less what happened at the pier. We've had our top investigators going over the scene, and I'll stand by the description they gave as to what happened."

Police believe that Spider-Man did survive the battle, since he was spotted swinging uptown by a patrol car later that evening. Attempts to get his attention and bring him in for questioning were ignored.

Fire fighters arrived on the scene at the pier and were able to put out several small fires, saving some of the remains of the warehouse so police scientists were able to go over it and try to determine the specifics

of the final Doc Ock/Spider-Man battle.

"If you ask me," said Captain DeWolff, "something huge went down here, and this city's safety was resting entirely on Spider-Man's shoulders. Fortunately for all of us, he was up to the job."

Authorities have been dragging the bottom of the river for some evidence of the machine or its creator. They have found several large chunks of it. Experts are even now studying them to try and determine exactly what the machine was designed to do. There have been no signs of Doc Ock himself, or even his four metal arms. Police suspect his drowned body may have floated out to sea.

When asked about the possibility that Doc Ock might have survived, DeWolff shuddered. "I certainly hope not. On the other hand, if he did," she said, smiling, "it's good to know we have Spider-Man to lend a hand."

THERE'S ONE BORN EVERY MINUTE

Editorial by J. Jonah Jameson

(Published May 1, 2004)

Showman P. T. Barnum was famous for saying, "There's a sucker born every minute."

Well, I can account for the whereabouts of quite a few of them.

They're in the letters to the editors that the *Daily Bugle* has received in recent days. Not only the ones we printed, but tons flooding in from dopey New Yorkers who all believe the same thing: Spider-Man is some sort of hero. That he wasn't in cahoots with Doc Ock (or, for that matter, the Green Goblin). That we in New York all owe him some sort of debt of gratitude.

Now Harry Osborn . . . he knows what's really going on. I spoke to him about it the other day. He grinned and said, "Spider-Man will be made to pay. Yes, he will!" And then he cackled and laughed like a total lunatic. That's my idea of a man with a head on his shoulders.

But the police, of all people! They should be out hunting him down, trying to throw handcuffs on his wrists, not flowers at his masked face. Even a reasonably intelligent woman like police detective Captain Jean DeWolff is going around singing his praises. "It's good to know we have Spider-Man to lend a hand," DeWolff told a *Bugle* reporter. Have the police gone insane? Has the whole town gone insane?

Let me put this in as clear and straight-forward a manner as I possibly can. Spider-Man is a menace. I know it, he knows it, and deep down you know it, too. He has to be. No one can be that noble, that caring, that good. No one can go around risking their lives time and again for no other reason than that they think they should. It's not plausible. He has some sort of angle. Some fiendish endgame. I may not have figured

out what it is yet, but I will.

In the meantime, for those of you who were born during the minute in between . . . don't let him fool you. Don't fall for his supposed heroics, or his daring swings down city streets. Never lose sight of the fact that Spider-Man is, and always will be, the most dangerous masked man in this city.

But this newspaper and I will always be there. We'll be watching for his tricks and continuing to warn you when we know he's up to something. Always know that the *Daily Bugle* is out to protect your interests. . . . even when someone like Spider-Man is threatening them.

OUT AND ABOUT

Who's Doing What, Where, and with Whom?!

By Rhoda Rooter

(Published May 2, 2004)

In some recent columns, I talked about the heartbreak that rising young actress Mary Jane Watson was going through, thanks to her being interested in a fellow who—incredibly—didn't seem to know a good thing when he had one.

Well, I'm happy to report that doesn't seem to be the case anymore. My little spies spotted Mary Jane and a brown-haired fellow dining at a downtown coffee shop. My spies only saw him from the back. She was all smiles, positively flirtatious. And the young man was no slouch either.

Naturally we want to leave them a *little* privacy. As near as my spies could overhear, though, the young man was saying something about his life once again being "a little more complicated," and that he wasn't going to be able "to be around as much as" he wanted.

Now I know what you're all thinking. Once again, for no understandable reason, our little Mary Jane is going to know heartbreak. Not so, I'm happy to admit! Because Mary Jane was apparently so full of cheer that you just wanted to shout, "Bring it on!" She pinned our unknown young fellow down on the issue of trying to be friends first and foremost . . . and letting everything else happen if and when it will.

Which, of course, is exactly the way you want to do it. Friends first, with everyone trying as hard as they can, and eventually coming together in the middle. All this reporter can say is that she's thrilled that everything appears to be working out for our redheaded heroine and her mysterious young man. I'm sure we'll be reading a lot more about them in the future!

And that's all this go-around from Rhoda!

HE'S FINALLY UNTANGLED

(Published May 3, 2004, in "Dear Lotta")

Dear Lotta:

I'm pretty sure this is the last time I'm going to be writing to you.

I took your advice, but then I "untook" it. Kind of.

I realize that, yes, I've got friends and family depending on me. But I have an extended family as well . . . the people of this city. I didn't know for the longest time how much the things I do mean to them. Now I do.

Deciding to help people wasn't an easy choice to make, but I did it once. I didn't realize it would be even harder the second time around. It was, though. Now that I've made it, I'll never lose sight of it again.

But I won't be losing sight of what I owe to those close to me, either. Anything in this

world—even a good thing—can be a bad thing if you make it your whole life. There's nothing wrong with devoting your life to good works. . . . as long as you don't make those who love you feel like they don't matter.

I've gone to one extreme and then the other, and I'm pretty sure I know how to keep the two halves of my life in line with each other. It's kind of like walking an incredibly thin line suspended between two buildings. But, believe it or not, I've gotten pretty good at balancing on lines exactly like that.

Thanks for all your help. . . .

Sincerely,

Untangled Web-Man

Dear Untangled Web-Man:

Good for you! I've been rooting for you all this time, and I'm thrilled you've finally got everything sorted out. Best of luck.

—*Lotta*